Much
Lov and
Gratitude!
~ christy Ann Edwards.

God Bless You!
Lou Johnson

The Night I Met Santa

Lora Johnson

Illustrated by Christine Ann Edwards

Book production by Lookout Design, Inc., Stillwater, MN 55082

www.lookoutdesign.com

Published by NLJ Books, Oak Grove, MN 55303

Printed in China

ISBN 978-1-60461-069-7

www.thenightimetsanta.com

www.lorajohnson.com

This Book is Dedicated to

Isaiah Daniel

It was Christmas Eve. Jeremy was lying awake in his bed struggling with the thoughts that kept him from sleeping.

That day had been a hard one! For some reason Jeremy was just down right ornery and had taken it out on his little brother. When Mom found out that he had socked Sam in the nose, she took down his stocking from the fireplace and sent him to his room. Dad soon followed, giving Jeremy "the talk" and his due discipline. Sam forgave him, and the day went on. However, Mom had not put his stocking back up. "I'm sure that Santa won't reward your bad behavior" she said. Jeremy chuckled and replied, loud enough for his little brother and sister to hear, "Oh, whatever Mom. There is no such thing as Santa Claus anyway."

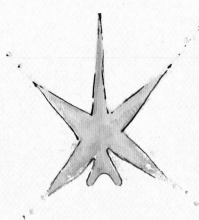

Recalling the days events, Jeremy wondered if he was right. What if he wasn't? What if there really was a Santa, and in the morning Sam and Jessica would have tons of presents, and he'd have none? "Oh, what does Mom know, anyway?" he thought. "I've done bad things before. I say I'm sorry, they say it's okay, and life goes on. I'll still get some stuff."

"Or will I?"

Just then Jeremy's thoughts were interrupted by a noise from downstairs. He sucked in his breath, lay as still as possible and listened. There! He heard it again. Someone was downstairs! Slowly Jeremy climbed out of bed and as quietly as possible crept down the stairs. When he reached the bottom step, he slowly peered around the corner into the living room and gasped at what he saw—Santa Claus! Jeremy fell backward and sat on the step with a quiet but definite thud. Nervously, Jeremy peered around the corner again, hoping that Santa hadn't heard him. Whew! He hadn't.

Santa stepped away from the fireplace where he had filled the stockings. Jeremy noticed a doll sticking out of Jessica's stocking, a dinosaur from Sam's, and, Yes! A new stocking was hanging where Jeremy's old one had been. "I knew it!" Jeremy smiled. "I knew Mom was wrong," he said as he started climbing the stairs.

"*Jeremy,*" *the deep voice resonated in his ears,* "Come here, Son." Jeremy turned slowly and saw the stern look on Santa's face, but as he walked closer he noticed a softness in Santa's eyes that comforted him. Santa sat down on the sofa and with strong, but gentle arms reached out and sat Jeremy next to him.

"Jeremy, you know that your Mom was right, don't you?"

"What do you mean, Santa?"

"Your stocking, and presents… Your Mother was right. You don't deserve them!"

"Are you taking them away from me?"

"Goodness no, Jeremy," Santa smiled.

"However, there is something you need to understand. These gifts I've given to you are not a reward. You've not been a very good young man!"

"I know" said Jeremy, all the pride he felt earlier in the evening vanishing in an instant. In its place a heavy heart tugged at his chest.

"Oh, come now Son, I didn't sit you down here to burden you."

"Santa, why did you bring me presents?"

"Ahhh, the question I hoped you'd ask. Let me tell you a story to help answer your question."

"*Long ago,* I too was a young man. A young man who thought that my parents were always wrong, and that the world revolved around me. One particular day, I found myself standing in a crowd, attracted to it because of the shouting and yelling. I was sure a fight was going on and wanted to get a look. When I finally made my way to the front of the crowd, I couldn't believe my eyes! A man carrying a cross was coming towards me from down the street. My initial thought was that this man was a thief or a criminal, and I started to shout at him myself. But then he got close enough for me to recognize him. The man was Jesus."

"Jesus!" said Jeremy. "You saw Jesus?"

"Yes, I did" nodded Santa.

"Gosh," Jeremy sat back as if exhausted, but eagerly he sat up again, anxious to hear more. "Did you know him?"

"Oh, a little" said Santa. I didn't know him as well as I knew of him."

About two weeks before this day, I had met Jesus. I was walking down the road during a really bad day when suddenly I noticed someone beside me. I looked over and saw that it was Jesus. Now, Jesus was famous! He was the miracle worker that everyone was talking about, and me… I was nobody special."

"But you're Santa!"

"Yes, I am now. But back then, I was nobody special. At least that is what I thought. So, I was quite taken by surprise!"

"Kind of like me, when I saw you?" asked Jeremy

"Very much like you."

"*Jesus spoke my name,*" said Santa.

"Jesus knew who I was. He told me that he had been looking for me because of my morning prayer. He said he had come to take away my burdens and asked me if I would give them to him, but I didn't know how. Jesus had smiled and said that I simply needed to tell him what they were and agree to let him have them."

"What did you do?"

"Well, I did just that. I told Jesus everything, and asked him if I'd ever be forgiven."

"What happened next?"

"Jesus hugged me and whispered, 'You are forgiven.' The weight in my chest disappeared in an instant, and I fell to the ground in relief. When I looked up, Jesus was gone."

"What did Jesus do with your burdens?"

"Well, Jeremy, when Jesus walked by me on that street, carrying that cross… I saw them. My burdens were nailed to the cross. But mine weren't the only ones there. I saw yours."

"Mine?!"

"I saw yours, mine… I saw everyone's burdens on that cross."

"How could Jesus carry all of those burdens? Why did he do it, Santa? Why?"

"Because, Jeremy, God had sent Jesus to Earth to take

away the sin of the world… to take our burdens from us so that he would be punished and not us."

"Jesus was punished?"

"Yes, Jeremy! Jesus was hung up to die on that cross he carried."

"But Santa, why? Why would God send Jesus to do that?"

"Because he loves us! He didn't want us to suffer, so he sent Jesus to go in our place."

"Gosh, Santa, Jesus died. . .for us?"

"Yes." Santa paused, "but for only three days."

"For only three days? How can that be?"

"Ahhh, a story for another time. I've kept you up way to late as it is."

"But Santa, how does this story answer my question? I still don't understand why you brought me presents."

"Well, Son, I didn't deserve to have Jesus take those burdens from me, and I knew it. But I was so grateful he had! I promised on that day that I would do everything I could to remind people what a wonderful gift Jesus Christ was to us. So, since Christmas is Jesus' Birthday, I travel to homes giving gifts, birthday gifts, even to little boys and girls who don't deserve them."

Jeremy was silent, digesting everything he had heard.

Santa scooped him up, carried him upstairs, and tucked him in to his bed.

"Santa, are you an angel?" Jeremy asked.

"Hmmm, of a sort, I suppose. I like to refer to myself as 'Gods Servant'."

"Santa?" Jeremy said sleepily.

"Yes, Jeremy?"

"Thank you."

"Ah, you're welcome Son. Don't forget to thank Jesus!"

"How Santa?"

"Just fold your hands and pray. He'll always be with you. He'll always hear you! God Bless you, Son!"

Jeremy woke up the next morning to squeals of delight ringing from his little sister. He ran downstairs, where he saw a stocking full and presents under the tree. But what caught his attention like never before was a small stable. Within that stable was the figure of a baby who had grown up to die in place of him.

This baby was Jesus.

The End

Santa's Prayer

Author unknown

The sleigh was all packed, the reindeer were fed,

But Santa still knelt by the side of the bed.

"Dear Father," he prayed "Be with me tonight.

There's much work to do and my schedule is tight.

I must jump in my sleigh and streak through the sky,

Knowing full well that reindeer can't fly.

I will visit each household before the first light,

I'll cover the world and all in one night,

With sleigh bells a-ringing, I'll land on each roof,

Amid the soft clatter of each little hoof.

To get in the house is the difficult part,

So I'll slide down the chimney of each child's heart.

My sack will hold toys to grant all their wishes.

The supply will be endless like the loaves and the fishes.

I will fill all the stockings and not leave a track.

I'll eat every cookie that is left for my snack.

I can do all these things Lord, only through you,

I just need your blessing, then it's easy to do.

All this is to honor the birth of the One,

That was sent to redeem us, Your most Holy Son.

So to all of my friends, least your glory I rob,

Please Lord, remind them who gave me this job.

How This Story Came to Be

Many people have asked and been inspired with how *The Night I Met Santa* came to be, and therefore I have for you another story… The story behind this book.

My oldest son, Isaiah, who had just turned four years old, suddenly began to think that he should be able to tell Mommy what to do rather than the other way around. All of you Mom's out there can imagine the frustration I was experiencing with a very strong willed four year old, who strives to be in control. About a week before Christmas, I was all out of patience, and in reaction mode took down his stocking. Meanwhile, I ensured him that all that I knew of Santa indicated that nothing would be found in his stocking or under the Christmas tree due to his naughtiness. With Isaiah crying in his room, his stocking in my hand, I sat on the edge of my bed asking God, "What now? I don't want to go through with this. His disappointment will overpower the joy in all of us… but how can I reward his behavior and expect it to change?" God answered me by saying, "Lora, Christmas is all about getting the Gift we never deserved, and never will."

Whoa….

Isaiah woke up to a stocking full and presents under the tree. He also woke up to an understanding that the greatest gift he ever received happened long ago; beginning with the birth of a baby who grew up, suffered, and then died… for him, for me, for you. The amazing effect of being able to correlate the grace involved with putting his stocking back up because of the Christmas and Easter Story, had an incredible impact on Isaiah! Amazing what God can do even in the fallibility of a mother at her wits end.

Soon after Christmas, I told my husband, Neil, that I felt God calling me to write a children's book. The book would bring the Grace of God and the gifts from Santa together, as we had experienced in our family that year. Neil's excitement was overwhelming. What also encouraged me to write the book was the many responses I received from friends and family who had read the "Naughty Story" in our Christmas letter that year.

For the next six months I slept with a notepad and pen on my night stand. Slowly, but surely the book came to me, different than what I had originally thought it would be like, but so much better than I had ever hoped. It is my prayer that this story will bless you!

Acknowledgements

To Rick and Suzy Roiger: Thank you for enduring the constant
interruptions and the night that never ended to edit this book. I Love You!

To Neil: This would have never happened without you.
Yet again, you've made another dream come true. I Love You says too
little... you are my Warrior. Thank you!

To My Heavenly Father: Thank you for choosing me to write this story.